DISNEY'S
MULAN

Adapted by Kathleen W. Zoehfeld

Layout drawings by Judith Holmes Clarke
Cleanup drawings by Denise Shimabukuro, Scott Tilley, and Lori Tyminski
Watercolors by Rae Ecklund, Robert Steele, and Brent Ford

DISNEY
PRESS

New York

Long ago in China, an important day in a girl's life was the day she presented herself to the matchmaker, who would arrange her marriage. This was Mulan's big day—the day she was to bring honor to her family. And she had bungled it, completely!

Mulan led her horse, Khan, solemnly home. As he drank from his trough, she studied her reflection in the water. "I'll never bring honor to my family," she sighed. "The other girls were quiet and demure—poised and polite. But me? I spoke without permission; spilled the tea! Even the cricket Grandmother Fa gave me couldn't bring enough luck."

Mulan slumped on the bench beneath the blossoming trees in the garden. From the doorway of the house, her father, Fa Zhou, watched her sadly.

"What beautiful blossoms we have this year," he said, sitting down beside her. He pointed to a pink and white bud. "Look. This one's late. But I'll bet when it blooms, it will be the most beautiful of all."

Her father took Mulan's hair comb from her hands and set it lovingly in her hair. Mulan smiled, the sadness disappearing from her eyes.

In the distance, they heard the village drummer announcing important visitors. Fa Zhou and Mulan, accompanied by her mother and grandmother, hurried to see what was happening.

The emperor's aide, Chi Fu, cried out: "Citizens! The Huns have invaded China! One man from every family must serve in the Imperial Army."

Oh, no! thought Mulan. Father is the only man in the Fa family. But his leg is injured. When the Fa name was called, Fa Zhou handed his cane to his wife and proudly took his conscription notice from the emperor's aide.

"No!" pleaded Mulan. "Please, sir—my father has already fought bravely for the emperor—"

"Silence!" interrupted Chi Fu, angry that a woman had spoken in the presence of men. "Mulan," whispered Fa Zhou. "You dishonor me."

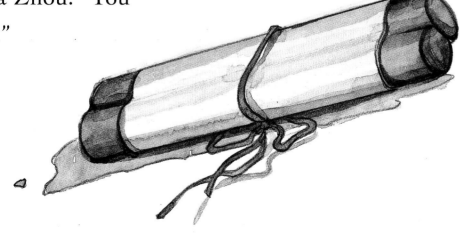

That evening, Mulan watched her father as he went to his armor cabinet. He lifted his sword gracefully—swung it high above his head and lunged forward. "Aagh!" he cried. Pain shot through his leg, and he crumpled to the floor.

Mulan rushed outside to the garden, fighting back her tears. She sat at the base of the Great Stone Dragon. A cold rain pelted the dragon's stony face. "I won't just sit by and let Father go to his death," she cried.

Inside the family temple, Mulan lit a stick of incense and placed it in the little dragon incense burner. "Please help me save Father's life," she prayed.

Mulan crept into the room where her parents were sleeping and set her comb on her father's table in exchange for his conscription notice. Then, she took his sword from the cabinet and cut her long black hair. She donned his armor, mounted Khan, and together they thundered out through the gate.

Awakening with a start, Grandmother Fa sat bolt upright in bed. "Mulan is gone!" she cried.

Fa Zhou awoke, bewildered. He noticed the hair comb on his table. He stumbled to his closet—his armor was missing!

"Mulan!" he shouted, as he threw open the front door.

"Go after her!" cried Fa Li. "She could be killed!"

"If I reveal her, she will be!" gasped Fa Zhou.

"Ancestors, hear our prayer," whispered Grandmother Fa. "Watch over Mulan."

At Grandmother Fa's words, the spirit of the First Ancestor took shape and cried, "Mushu, awaken!"

The dragon incense burner's metal body trembled. "I live!"

"Mushu!" thundered the First Ancestor. "Awaken the ancestors!"

Mushu sighed and clanged his gong. The temple soon filled with the chatter of ancestral spirits. "We must send a guardian to bring Mulan back," said one.

"Yes!" they all agreed. "Send the most powerful of all!"

"Okay, okay," said Mushu, "I'll go."

The ancestors roared with laughter. "After all the trouble you caused last time!? You'll never be a guardian again!"

"Go. Awaken the Great Stone Dragon!" ordered the First Ancestor. And he threw Mushu out the door.

"Rocky! Wake up!" cried Mushu. He banged his gong. Nothing. He hit the statue with his gong, and the stone crumbled.

"Great Stone Dragon, have you awakened?" called the First Ancestor.

Mushu emerged from the rubble, holding the dragon's head before him. "I, ah . . . yes. I am the Great Stone Dragon!"

"Go!" said the First Ancestor. "The fate of the Fa family rests in your claws."

"That's just great," sighed Mushu. "I'm doomed!"

Grandmother Fa's cricket, Cri-Kee, chirped encouragingly.

"I've got it!" Mushu cried. "I'll make Mulan a hero! Then the ancestors will have to give me my job back!" He quickly set out after Mulan with Cri-Kee close behind.

By early morning, Mulan had reached a hilltop overlooking the Imperial Army camp. "I'd better get some practice," she told Khan. She took a manly stance and drew her sword. It snagged on its scabbard and clattered to the ground. "It's going to take a miracle to get me into the army," she sighed.

Suddenly, a great, towering shadow was cast upon the rocks nearby. "Did I hear someone ask for a miracle!?" it roared.

"Who are you?" gasped Mulan in awe.

"Who am I? Your guardian," cried Mushu. "I have been sent by your ancestors to guide you through your masquerade!" He stepped out from behind the rock that had hidden him.

"My ancestors sent a lizard to help me?" she asked.

"Dragon," corrected Mushu. He and Cri-Kee hid inside Mulan's kerchief. "Let's get this show on the road!" he said.

Mulan walked awkwardly through the crowded army camp.

"Try to act like them," coached Mushu. Mulan strode up to a group of three soldiers: Yao, Chien-Po, and Ling.

"Punch him," Mushu whispered to Mulan. "It's how men say hello."

Mulan hit Yao on the shoulder.

"Grrrr," growled Yao. "You ain't worth my time, chicken boy!"

"Say that to my face, ya limp noodle!" cried Mushu from inside Mulan's kerchief. Mulan cringed.

Yao turned and swung a punch. Mulan ducked, and Yao's fist landed on Ling's jaw instead. General Li and his son, Captain Shang, and the emperor's aide, Chi Fu, stepped out of the command tent and saw the chaos.

"When you have trained these recruits, you will join us. Good luck, Captain," said the general.

The next morning, Captain Shang began training the new recruits. He shot an arrow into the top of a tall pole. "Yao. Retrieve the arrow," he commanded. "But wait! You seem to be missing something." He opened a box, took out two heavy bronze disks, and tied them to Yao's wrists. "The first one represents discipline," he said. "The second, strength."

Yao and the other soldiers tried to reach the arrow and failed. Then Shang put them through maneuver after maneuver.

After several days, Mulan's gaze caught the arrow lodged atop the pole. And an idea came to her. Instead of allowing the heavy disks to dangle down and hinder her ascent, she would use them to help her. Quickly she tied the disks together and used them to counter her weight as she shinnied up the pole.

"Hooray!" shouted the soldiers as Mulan held up the arrow in triumph.

Still, Chi Fu wasn't impressed. "Those boys aren't fit to be soldiers," he said to Shang. "When I send your father, the general, my report, your troops will never see battle."

Mushu was listening. "Oh, no," he groaned. "How am I going to make Mulan a hero if she doesn't fight?" He snuck inside Chi Fu's tent and made Cri-Kee forge an official letter. Then he patched together a soldier puppet with some leftover armor, set it on a panda, and rode it up to Chi Fu.

"Urgent letter from General Li," said the puppet.

"Who are you?" asked Chi Fu suspiciously.

"We're in a war, man!" cried the puppet. "There's no time for stupid questions!" He handed Chi Fu the letter.

"Captain!" shouted Chi Fu, reading its contents. "We're needed at the front!"

Shang gathered his troops, and they trudged up the snowy slopes toward the Tung-Shao Pass. In the distance, they spied a plume of black smoke. As they approached, they could see a village in ruins.

"I don't understand," said Shang. "My father should have been here."

Chi Fu pointed to the valley below. The Imperial forces lay defeated—all, including the general, dead.

"I'm sorry," whispered Mulan.

Shang roused his courage. "The Huns are moving quickly," he said. "We'll make better time to the Imperial City if we go through the pass. We're the only hope for the emperor now. Move out!"

As the soldiers forged through the pass, an arrow thunked Shang's armor and knocked him off his horse. Suddenly, a hail of flaming arrows filled the air. The Huns were attacking!

"Get out of range!" shouted Shang. "Save the cannons!" They retreated behind a line of rocks and began to fire the cannons at the Huns.

"Heeiiaahh!!!" came the bloodcurdling cry of the Hun leader, Shan-Yu, as he led the charge down the mountainside.

"Hold the last cannon for Shan-Yu!" cried Shang.

The soldiers drew their swords, ready for battle. Mulan studied the mountain crest reflected in her blade. She grabbed the last cannon and charged toward the Huns alone.

"Come back!" cried Shang.

Mulan planted the cannon and aimed. She yanked on Mushu's tail. *Whoosh*—a little flame leaped out of his mouth and lighted the fuse. *Kaboom!* The rocket zoomed well over Shan-Yu's head.

"You missed him," nagged Mushu. "How could you miss him?!"

Wham! The rocket slammed into the mountaintop and exploded, sending an avalanche of snow roaring down. Shan-Yu lashed his sword at Mulan in fury. She jumped away and stumbled through the snow, trying to outrun the avalanche. She was losing the race! But so was Shan-Yu.

"Auggghhh!!!" Mulan heard Shan-Yu and his Huns cry out as the avalanche buried them.

In the nick of time, Khan raced to Mulan's rescue, and she vaulted onto his back. Then they spotted Shang, caught in waves of onrushing snow. Mulan lifted him out of the avalanche's grip, and Khan carried them both to safety. When they had all reached higher ground, the troops gathered around Mulan and cheered.

"You are the craziest man I've ever met," said Shang. "And for that I owe you my life. From now on, you have my trust."

"Aaah," groaned Mulan. She felt her aching side. Her hand was covered in blood.

"He's injured!" cried Shang. "Get him to the medic's tent!"

After tending Mulan's

wound, the medic stepped outside. Mulan's secret was revealed.

"A woman! Treacherous snake!" cried Chi Fu.

"I did it to save my father," she explained to Shang.

"High treason!" cried Chi Fu. "Captain? You know what must be done."

Shang threw Mulan's sword in the snow before her. "A life for a life," he said. "My debt is repaid." Then, turning to the troops he cried, "Move out!"

Chi Fu sputtered in disbelief. "By law she must be put to death!"

But Shang had made his decision. He glared at Chi Fu. "I said, move out!"

As the troops vanished into the snowy pass, Mulan sighed. "I should never have left home."

"Hey," said Mushu. "You did it to save your father's life."

"Maybe I didn't go for my father," said Mulan. "Maybe what I really wanted was to prove I could do things right."

"The truth is, we're both frauds," said Mushu. "Your ancestors never sent me. You risked your life to help people you love. I risked your life to help myself."

"Well, let's go home," sighed Mulan.

An eerie howl stopped them in their tracks. They crept to the edge of a cliff and peered down. Shan-Yu had smashed out of his icy grave. Soon, his five strongest Huns joined him!

"They're heading for the Imperial City," gasped Mulan. "I have to do something!"

Mulan galloped through the city gates, with Mushu and Cri-Kee beside her.

"The Huns are here!!" she cried, when she had finally caught up with her comrades.

"Why should I believe you?" said Shang. He turned away and climbed the great stairs toward the emperor.

Mulan watched as the emperor proclaimed victory. Suddenly, the Huns burst out of a paper dragon, knocked Shang to the ground, and carried the emperor up to the tower. Shang rallied his men and tried to batter down the palace door.

"You'll never get in that way," Mulan called. "Come with me."

Shang stared at her stubbornly. Yao, Ling, and Chien-Po took off after Mulan.

Mulan led them to a quiet spot, where she disguised them as women. Then, following Mulan's lead, each one removed his sash and wrapped it around one of the palace pillars. Shang saw what they were doing. He took off his cape and joined them as they shinnied up.

Inside, they found the Huns guarding a door. Mulan and her "girls" took the guards by surprise and overpowered them. With the guards out cold, Shang burst though the door. He saw Shan-Yu's sword poised over the emperor's head.

Shang charged toward Shan-Yu and fought him off, while Mulan helped Ling, Yao, and Chien-Po get the emperor to safety along a zip-line of banners.

Mulan cut the zip-line so Shan-Yu could not follow the emperor.

"Nooo!" cried Shan-Yu. He turned to Mulan in fury. Mulan grabbed Mushu and fled.

"What's the plan?" asked Mushu.

Mulan pointed to the fireworks tower.

"I'm way ahead of you," Mushu replied. He and Cri-Kee hopped on a kite and flew to the tower.

By the time Mushu returned with a rocket strapped to his back, Mulan had led Shan-Yu to the roof. The huge Hun lunged for her, but she dodged his blow. As he teetered, off-balance, she kicked his legs out from under him and pinned him to the roof with his own sword.

Seeing the opportunity, Mushu lighted a little stick and handed it to Cri-Kee. "Light me!" he cried, pointing to the fuse. *Woosh!* Mushu guided the rocket toward Shan-Yu. Mulan ducked.

"Aggghhh!" cried Shan-Yu as the rocket carried him off to crash into the fireworks tower. *Kaablaaam!*

Propelled by the blast, Mulan fell down the stairs and landed on Shang. Mushu and Cri-Kee crash-landed nearby.

"Fa Mulan," said the emperor, "you have saved us all. And for that, I honor you." He bowed to her.

Everyone began to bow and cheer.

The emperor placed his pendant around Mulan's neck. "Take this," he said, "so your family will know what you have done for me." He handed her Shan-Yu's sword. "And this, so the world will know what you have done for China."

Mulan returned home. She knelt before her father and presented the emperor's gifts of honor. Fa Zhou took them solemnly and set them aside. "The greatest gift and honor is having you for a daughter. I have missed you so."

"I've missed you, too," she said.

"Isn't it wonderful," sighed Fa Li.

"Great," said Grandmother Fa, "she brings home a sword, but if you ask me, she should have brought home a ma . . ."

"Excuse me," called Shang, passing through the gate. "Does Fa Mulan live here? Oh . . . Mulan. I have come to . . . uh . . . return your helmet. That is, er . . . your father's helmet," he stammered.

Mulan and her father exchanged a smile.

"Shang," she asked, "would you like to stay for dinner?"

In the temple, the First Ancestor leaned out the window, watching.

"Well," said Mushu, "c'mon . . . who did a good job? Who?"

"Oh, all right," muttered the First Ancestor. "You can be a guardian again."

"Yaaaahhhh!!!" cried Mushu. "Guess who's back on pedestal five!"

Cri-Kee banged the gong in glee, and the ancestors cheered.

Everyone celebrated a happy ending to Mulan and Mushu's adventures.

Printed in the United States of America.
First Edition
1 3 5 7 9 10 8 6 4 2
ISBN: 0-7868-3172-3 (trade) 0-7868-5064-7 (lib. bdg.)
Library of Congress Cataloging in Publication Card Number 97-80162
This book is set in 18-point Cochin.

For more Disney Press Fun, visit www.DisneyBooks.com

Actual images from the film were not used to illustrate this book. Instead, a team of Disney character artists worked together to bring to life the story of Mulan, using art references from the Walt Disney Feature Animation division. The illustrations were created in a fashion similar to that used by Disney animation artists in creating the actual film.

Initial layouts of each piece of book artwork were drawn in pencil. These loose layouts showed the character as well as the background of each scene to be depicted. Several drafts of these layouts were drawn to ensure that the text and the artwork worked together to best convey the story. Also, the layout artist focused on visual storytelling, rather than how precisely the line was drawn. This task fell to the cleanup pencil artists.

Once the pencil drawings were finalized, cleanup drawings were created. These tight pen-and-ink drawings are still visible in the finished artwork. However, the color was added by the watercolorists. These artists took the cleanup book artwork and the color palette developed by Walt Disney Feature Animation for the film, *Mulan*, and brought to vivid life the film's story.